Fairy Finders

A Short Story By

R C Dean

Published by  Publishing

Published by *FaRoosi*[®] Publishing
© Faroosi Publishing
The moral rights of the author have been asserted

First published 2015
First Edition

ISBN 978-0-9933698-1-0

Written by
R C Dean □ □

Chapter 1

When Clara woke up, the house was quieter than usual. Beams of beige autumn light were shining through cracks in the curtain. She wasn't sure if it was morning or night. Her mother wasn't in the bedroom and neither was the leather bag with the paraffin and matches.

She could hear the postman's bike coming round the corner, the fireworks must have stopped. She lifted herself out of bed and gazed out of the window. Everything was normal. The same postman, same bike – nothing had changed. She closed the window, sighed and walked off towards the kitchen.

Mother was frying eggs on the stove and boiling water in the kettle. Father was lying down on the sofa with his newspaper. He was clearly tired but he still looked smart in his grey suit with his hair neatly combed back.

Clara's dad sat down next to her.

"Your hamsters are sleeping. Gracie was still shocked from the firework display last night but I kept stroking her until she dozed off. The garden is a mess, if they carry on letting these fireworks land in people's gardens, there'll be no flowers left."

"It won't look like a *garden* without the flowers," her mother sighed weakly. For she had been working on their garden for years now and it would indeed not look like a garden if it was ruined. "Eat your breakfast now before it gets cold" she said in her usual motherly way, trying to cheer up. Clara didn't need to be asked again as fried eggs were a once in a blue moon treat as far as she was concerned. She ate her breakfast greedily and listened to her parents' conversation. She found that she heard much more conversation if she stayed silent.

 "I thought that I would never sleep last night, honestly. That Catherine wheel nearly burned a hole in the roof!"

"It wasn't a Catherine wheel," exclaimed Father grandly. "It was a roman candle. It came right over the house and crashed on the allotments in town." Mother looked worried.

"Don't worry dear, nobody was there, no one ever is. After all, it's just a pile of yellow grass and dead pansies."

Clara wolfed down the last of her breakfast and pleaded with her father.

"Please may I see them?"

"I suppose so, but it's nothing but a pile of rubble now."

Mother was concerned. "Will it be safe?"

"Of course it will, there's nothing there."

"No more fireworks".

"Trust me, it will be fine."

"Can I take the old picnic basket and the broom?" asked Clara.

"Alright but make sure you clean them afterwards and be careful when you come back, don't spill any gunpowder on the patio."

Every year in November, the council would hold a fireworks display and the day afterwards, all of the children would collect the coloured gunpowder off the streets and mix it with paraffin to create candles which gave off impressive coloured flames.

Clara made the second best candles in her neighbourhood. All the other children tried to find things on the pavements and roads but anything there would be taken or blown away by the wind.

The trick was to look in grassy, bushy areas. She walked along the long, winding narrow streets, her beady eyes scanning every corner of the path. In the tiniest corner of the road, she spotted a lovely heap of turquoise powder from a Catherine wheel and brushed it into her basket, carefully separating it from the yellow she had found earlier.

But she had 7 candles which gave off the same coloured glow as this. Elizabeth Smith had 10. Elizabeth had the best collection of candles in the neighbourhood. Everybody agreed. No one was quite sure until Elizabeth found a roman candle which, when made into a candle, gave off an impressive, 10cm high, purple glow with green sparks. Clara's smile faded.

 She knew that 1000 Catherine wheels couldn't beat a roman candle. She sat down and tried to remember the fireworks from last night and where they landed. It was funny though because she couldn't remember anything apart from the time when a yellow Catherine wheel went off, she could have sworn that one of the stars in the sky disappeared, but when she tried to tell her parents they didn't believe it.

"Just a trick of the firework light" replied her mother wearily.

The street was a complete mess of charcoal-grey ash and coloured power. A heap of orange powder was in the garden of a house that had a stain on one of its walls from the gunpowder. The people who lived in the house were rushing in and out of the house with bottles of lavender paraffin from the bathroom and spilling it lightly over the gunpowder to create more fireworks.

More bright ash was being swept away by the caretaker Mr Rowan. He was wearing his usual shabby overalls and tatty cap tipped at a jaunty angle. He claimed he was just doing his job by cleaning the streets but everybody knew the real reason why he swept the streets. He would collect the gunpowder and sell it to candle makers.

Clara gasped. This ash was from the Chinese Crackers that went off the night before. If only she could get it. It would make a candle 100 times better than Elizabeth's. But how could she make Mr Rowan go away?

An idea flashed in her head. She ripped the bottom of her dress and sprinkled some of the turquoise powder on her shoulders. She ran to the caretaker, screaming.

"Mr R, Mr R! There's a massive pile of yellow gunpowder and my father accidently dropped our paraffin lamp on top of it and there are massive flames, they look like the ivory fountain that went off last night!"

Mr Rowan had a greedy look on his face. Chinese Crackers were nothing compared to the ivory fountain that took place the night before.

"Come on show me, show me!"

"I'm sorry but mother said I mustn't go back. She is worried it's not safe, but I can tell you the address." She told the caretaker the address of the house with the orange fireworks and in the blink of an eye, he was off towards the direction of the house, the pockets on his overalls flapping in the wind.

Clara gazed at the pile of pink gunpowder. She tried to sweep it into her basket but there was more than she expected. A gust of wind came out of nowhere and blew away practically all of it. It wasn't worth having anymore.

All of a sudden, she heard an angry scream coming from the distance. Mr R was back. Clara leapt up and ran towards the woods.

The woods were dark and had several unpleasant smells. No one ever went into them, however Clara felt that they were mysterious and magical and liked it that way. As she walked on through the thick grass, damp with dew, she saw a peculiar glow, coming from the end of the woods. As she ventured deeper, the light grew stronger and she could see a pile of green powder on top of the muddy bank.

Clara pushed her way through the leaves and saw it clearly. It was the gunpowder from the Catherine wheel from last night. She didn't know whether to bother collecting the powder. It wasn't a particularly a special Catherine wheel.

Then she noticed something. There, sitting on top of the gunpowder was a creamy white sphere - a bit like a pearl. It seemed to be the thing that was creating the light.

Could it possibly be? Was it the... star?

Chapter 2

Clara tried to climb onto the heap of gunpowder but it just tumbled down through her fingers. She tried again and again but she couldn't get to the top. She balanced her broom in front of the heap and stepped on it as if it were a staircase. She peered over the top and gasped.

Lying there, with one arm stretched over the star, was what looked like... A fairy! Clara was worried, and then the truth struck her. The fairy was dead. She didn't know whether to be relieved or frightened. It was as if the gunpowder had crawled into her stomach and was exploding inside her. She could not bring herself to take the star.

Then she looked at her watch. Mother had told her to be back by 9:00pm. It was 9:45pm. Clara grabbed her basket and rushed home to find Mother, white as a ghost, standing at the doorstep.

"Oh thank goodness you're alright. What were you playing at? I was worried sick!"

"Sorry Mum, I didn't realize what time it was. I just... passed our new neighbour, he was really chatty, honest, but I didn't want to seem rude."

"Well at least you're all right now. Where's the broom? I need to sweep the kitchen."

Oh no! She had forgotten it in the woods, in front of the gunpowder, but she didn't want to tell mother that she had been there.

"I... er... let our new neighbour borrow it. He had lots of ash in his garden, but I'll get it back later, I promise."

The rest of the day was reasonably peaceful, however Clara thought about the fairy throughout the whole of it. It was strange because half of her was sick with fear and the other half was filled with curiosity, an urge to get the star, but no matter how intrigued she was, she was deathly pale for the whole of the evening.

"Would you like me to help you make your candles?" Clara's dad asked eagerly. "I went to the shop and bought 5 new slabs of paraffin and a box of matches."

But Clara was so busy thinking about the fairy, she didn't hear him.

"You're awfully pale, I wonder if we should take you to the hospital?"

"No dad, I'm alright, really. I didn't get any sleep last night because of the fireworks, in fact I'll go and have a nap now."

She ran upstairs, but instead of going to her room, she climbed up into the attic. She couldn't possibly carry the star herself. By the looks of things, the star was very heavy, maybe she could use Mother's gardening spade. That would do the job.

At 10:30pm, when she knew that her parents were asleep, she grabbed a candle and the spade and tiptoed out of the house.

The street seemed mysterious at night. The roads seemed longer, the trees seemed blacker and everything was silent. The woods were especially frightening. Every tiny noise, like a gust of wind or a flock of birds made Clara jump and seemed to make her more cautious every time.

Eventually, she reached the clearing. She lit the candle and held it up to her face. There was the broom, the green powder, the star and the fairy. Shaking, she climbed onto the broom and reached out for the star.

It slowly began to slip down the gunpowder and onto Clara's hand. She was about to leave, when she felt a longing to take the fairy as well. She knew it wasn't wise to tell anyone (she didn't intend to either) but she wanted to have it anyway. Gently, she pushed her hand towards the fairy and touched its cold hand. Like the star, the fairy slithered down the powdery slide and onto her hand. Clara placed it in her pocket carefully.

All of a sudden, a loud bang and a cascade of pink sparks went up in the air. It was her pink Catherine wheel candle that she had made the day before!

"Who's lighting fireworks?" a sharp, croaky voice roared from deep inside the woods. It was Mr Rowan on his night patrol. Clara ran out of the clearing, through the brambles and out of the woods, only to find the beastly Mr R waiting at the opening of the woods.

"What have we here?" the horrible caretaker cackled.

Still clutching the star in her sweaty hands, Clara quickly blew out her candle and silently ran as fast as she could, all the way home, desperately trying to avoid the Caretaker.

Chapter 3

Clara reached a familiar blue door. She was home. She grabbed the door handle, threw herself into the house and slammed the door behind her. She sighed with relief and tiptoed up into her room but Mother came through the door, still in her dressing gown.

"What on earth are you playing at, it's 1:00am!"

"Sorry Mum, I'll go to sleep now, look." Clara climbed into her small wooden bed and pulled her crisp, white duvet over her body.

"Wait, you need to put your pyjamas on. You can't sleep in those clothes - they're soaking wet!"

Reluctantly, Clara pulled off her muddy jeans and exchanged them for her fluffy pink pyjamas. She decided that when her mother had gone back to bed, she would tiptoe downstairs and retrieve the fairy and the star out of her pocket but she was so tired, she could barely lift herself out of bed.

The next morning, Clara rushed out of bed, slipped on her fluffy slippers and rushed outside to the garden. Clara's jeans were dripping with water.

She pulled the fairy and the star out of the pocket. The fairy had streaks of soap in her hair and the star was covered in soapy suds but other than that, they were fine.

Clara ran back into her room, still clutching the fairy in one hand, the star in the other. Carefully, she placed both the fairy and the star into her jewellery box and locked it. She slipped the key into her pocket.

It was tempting to take them into school, but it was too risky. Mr R would be there and so would the headmaster, she was bound to get found out.

Elizabeth was outside school. A huge crowd was gathering round her including Clara's best friend, Jane Thomas - or Plain Jane as most people called her (she wasn't particularly popular, especially with Elizabeth). Jane's mouth was wide open, like almost everybody else's.

"Eliza, Eliza- can I see?" someone called out. Elizabeth was holding a small candle.

"I wouldn't show off that lump of paraffin if I were you Liz" Clara remarked.

"Oh haha Clara Jones, take a look at this!"

She lit it with a match. The fire roared up into the air and out cascaded 5 tiny sparks.

Clara rolled her eyes and walked off.

"That's heaps better than your trashy Catherine wheels!" Elizabeth called after her.

Chapter 4

"Mrs Montgomery," Mr Bayne, the headmaster, yelled from behind the desk. Mr Bayne had been known throughout the whole school for his impatience, so Mrs Montgomery knew better than to keep him waiting.

"Yes Mr Bayne," she replied quickly

"We have a scientist, wanting to see you," he said flatly with a sarcastic grin on his face. "Please ensure this is quick because I actually have the common sense to want to get on with my life – in peace!" And with that, he stormed out of the room, clutching a pile of paperwork.

Mrs Montgomery sat down at the desk, patiently tapping her fingers on the glossy oak surface. A man wearing a white coat entered the room. He looked like a stranger yet he was so familiar.

"...Spencer- isn't it? Mr Spencer?" Mrs Montgomery asked.

"Yes, Mrs Montgomery." he replied, nodding his head.

"Well Mr Spencer, what can I do for you?"

"The local caretaker, Mr Rowan, has reported a child hanging around the local woods and thinks that something suspicious is going on," he began. "Lighting fireworks, walking round late at night and trying to trick him into bothering innocent locals - and he clearly isn't having any of it. It would be great if you could help me investigate."

Mrs Montgomery smiled.

"Ok, but please make sure it isn't too long - you know how impatient the headmaster is."

Mr Spencer suddenly turned quite pale.

"Are you ok Mr Spencer?" she asked, worried.

"Yes, just a bit shocked, I am alright, really, I just think it would be...um, a bit easier if I...er, showed you... Mrs Montgomery." Mr Spencer spluttered uneasily, "Would you have time to go down to the woods with me right now?"

"Of course, if that's what you would like Mr Spencer."

He hastily picked himself up, mopped his forehead with a handkerchief from his pocket and stumbled out of the room, Mrs Montgomery following behind him.

The journey to the woods was reasonably short but Mr Spencer didn't say a word throughout the whole of it, except a quick -

"Here we are," when they turned the corner of the pavement.

When they arrived at the woods, Mrs Montgomery noticed that the woods were not a very uplifting place but she seemed to sense something special about them. A path had formed where trees had burned down and a trail of pink powder littered the ground. Mrs Montgomery and Mr Spencer followed it until they reached a big heap of green powder.

"We traced down a white chalky substance mixed in this pile of Catherine Wheel ash and it appears to be identical to the substance on the surface of the moon." He whispered. "We think that some part of the solar system has fallen to earth but when we came in search for it, it had long gone. I reckon that some kid has got their grubby hands on it before we got a chance to look at it. We desperately need to find it."

"Are you suggesting that it's a pupil at my school?" Mrs Montgomery questioned.

"It is the closest school to these woods and we really need to take a closer look. It could unlock another secret to the universe!"

Chapter 5

"Hey," whispered Jane hoping that the teacher wouldn't see her. "A scientist came to school yesterday afternoon. He came to see Mr. Bayne. He took Mrs. Montgomery to the woods as well!"

"Do you know why?" asked Clara.

"Maybe she broke into Buckingham palace?" laughed Jane.

Clara laughed but she had a worried look on her face.

'What if they know about the star?' Clara thought to herself.

Jane knew that something wasn't right, but she tried to go along with it.

"Did you hear that Mrs. Wilson might get fired!" exclaimed Clara in an attempt to hide her worries and change the subject.

"Really, how did you find that out?" questioned Jane

"I overheard Elizabeth, she is such a blabber mouth," replied Clara. "Anyway, let's get on with our work."

The bell rang and Clara dashed off to the woods. When she got there, she hid her bag next to a tree so that no one could steal it. She then went to search for the gunpowder to investigate.

Clara checked to see if there was anyone there. But it was deserted. She knew that she was safe.

From out of nowhere, two large hands came and grabbed her from behind. "Help! Help! There is a kidnapper." She knew it was Mr. Rowan but she struggled and screamed anyway.

"Stop kicking me you imbecilic child! What are you doing here? I am no kidnapper! How dare you, repulsive girl!"

"Sorry Mr. Rowan." said Clara innocently.

"I should think so!" He said and continued "Well...?"

"Well what?" she replied and continued "I thought you were the kidnapper that captured the little girl last week."

"I don't know anything about that but what I do know is that I am not the kidnapper that you are thinking of, and if I find you here again you will be in big trouble!"

Clara went back to retrieve her bag and hurriedly ran back to the school as she did not want to be late and face the wrath of the cold hearted, cruel, menacing person that was Mr. Williams.

When Clara got back to school, her heart was pounding underneath her chequered pinafore. Not only was she tired, but she knew that she wasn't the only one who knew about the star.

Chapter 6

The crisp autumn air whirled around Clara's face. She pulled her coat tighter around her body and sat down on the nest of cushions she had plonked onto the grass.

"Can't we go inside now Jane?" Clara asked, shivering.

"Oh all right, if you insist."

Jane picked up her coat and followed Clara through the glass door and up the stairs into the messy mauve jungle that was Jane Thomas' bedroom. Jane threw herself onto the bed whilst Clara hurled herself at the armchair, resting peacefully in the corner of the room.

A ray of sunshine shot through the window, lighting up the whole room.

"C'mon Clara, it's sunny now- let's go explore. We can collect some gunpowder to make candles later - I bet we can find some ash that'll make Elizabeth's candles look like a bunch of broken light bulbs."

This time, Clara couldn't stop her. They wondered out into the street.

"It's cold." Clara moaned.

"Stop fussing. Look - is that roman candle ash over there?"

Clara knew that it was only from a Catherine Wheel but she sighed and hastily swept it into the basket all the same.

"Oh do cheer up," begged Jane, skipping around in the street. A striking white light burst though Clara's trouser pocket. She tried to cover it with her hands but it was too late.

"Oh my word Clara! What on earth was that?"

Clara sighed. She had been longing to tell someone about the star for weeks. She couldn't stop herself from telling Jane.

"I can't keep it a secret any longer Jane." Clara burst into tears. "A few weeks ago I went exploring in the woods. I knew that something wasn't right after the firework display but I didn't expect to find these." She pulled out the star and the fairy corpse from her pocket. Jane's eyes widened and she threw her hands at her mouth.

"A fairy?" Jane whispered.

"And I think this might be a star." Clara replied.

"This is incredible! Just think, Jane and Clara, fairy finders - star seekers! We'll be on the radio and..."

"No Jane, we're not telling anybody." Clara said firmly.

"But!"

"No."

The following week, Clara and Jane were walking back from school when Clara stopped for a moment.

"Jane look - it's Tricky Vicky. Maybe we can get friendly with her and build a den in her garden to keep the star safe. Nobody dares to knock on her door let alone climb into her garden, it will be safe and I can't leave it in my bedroom but I can't risk that glow coming from my pocket again." Clara said

"And we can't risk Vicky telling, or her mum finding out. Besides, you said it yourself, we're not telling anyone." Jane replied.

"Ok, let's go over to her but if she says no – we leave right now!" replied Jane.

Looking at Vicky, it was hard to distinguish that this was the girl who had anything that she wanted with the click of her little, stubby fingers. The girl who's family was possibly the wealthiest in the country and the girl who lived in the most posh three storey house in the town. She was swatting a fly with her exercise book.

 "Hey Vicky," Jane yelled impatiently. "Over here!"

"What would one like to enquire after oneself?" Vicky asked.

Jane was baffled.

"What?" she replied rather loudly. Clara could have died with embarrassment.

"She was asking what you wanted," she whispered in Jane's ear.

"Oh, so that's what she meant – how was I supposed to know?

"Anyway, let's just tell her about the star."

"Star! What star?" Vicky cried.

"Be quiet and then we'll explain." Jane whispered.

Jane explained everything that happened while Clara silently displayed the evidence.

Just as they were walking home, Clara noticed Elizabeth from the corner of her eye.

"What does she want," Jane muttered under her breath.

"Oh look! It's Clara know-it-all with a pair of monkeys – I didn't know the circus was coming to town today!"

Elizabeth and her friends erupted into laughter.

"Oh and look – the clown has just arrived!" Clara remarked.

"You think you're so clever, don't you? You strut around showing off your stupid candles and badmouthing everybody else." replied Elizabeth.

"Hmm, I'm sure that sounds like somebody else I know... You maybe?" Jane added.

"Stay out of it Plain Jane. Talking of plain, look at that little bracelet." Elizabeth seized it and held it out of her reach.

"Give it back!" Clara yelled and grabbed it back. Elizabeth was stunned.

You see, Clara had never stood up to her like that or shouted, and even Clara herself was shocked.

"Get lost and take your silly little flying pigs with you. Stay away from all three of us – okay!" Clara screamed and stormed off, Vicky and Jane following. Leaving Elizabeth and her friends in shock.

They stayed away from Clara for the rest of that week.

The week after, Jane's parents invited lots of family over for a party, to celebrate Mr Thomas' new job. Jane had asked Clara to come over and they were both thinking about the star.

"You know, it might be useful if we find out about space. I know Mr Brown makes it seem boring but it might come in handy." Clara said.

"That's it! My dad's brother is an astronaut, he's here today. We'll ask him about space – carefully of course, we don't want him knowing about the star. He might even write out some facts! It's worth a try."

So Clara and Jane tiptoed down the stairs and peeped around the door of the front room. They walked into the room with their notebooks and pencils and sat down next to Jane's uncle.

"Uncle Charles. We're learning about the solar system in school – Clara and I, would you care to tell us a little bit about it, please?"

Clara and Jane fluttered their eyelashes for Britain.

Charles Thomas knew that the secrets of space were forbidden to tell anyone but what harm would it do just revealing a few facts. He drew out a map of space for Clara and Jane.

Meanwhile, Clara's mum was tidying up the kitchen.

"Dear, have you seen the rug?" she asked her husband who was scoffing up some biscuits and reading the news.

"No, I haven't sorry."

Clara's mother was confused. Where had it gone?

Chapter 7

"Vicky, pass me a nail, there's a loose floorboard I need to hammer down," Jane yelled, yanking at the floor. Winter was approaching fast and Clara, Jane and Vicky had started building a den in the old, rickety shed that had been rumoured to have sat in Vicky's back garden since the Bronze Age. They had draped an old curtain over a few boxes to make a chair and patched up the broken windows with used cereal boxes. A rug from Clara's house lay on the tatty floor and the star and the fairy stood proudly on an old battered table. No one was allowed to touch them unless they got permission from Clara. After a lot of debating, the girls had decided that Clara was the most sensible and careful and therefor was elected 'leader'.

"Clara, can I go home now?" Jane begged.

"Oh all right. I need to do my homework anyway." replied Clara.

A week later, it was bonfire night and another firework display was about to begin.

"I can't wait until tonight!" exclaimed Clara. "It'll be fantastic!"

"Be careful and stay with Jane and Vicky," nagged Mrs Jones, Clara's mum and for once Clara wasn't listening. She was too busy thinking about the fireworks.

Meanwhile, in the park, Jane was waiting for the other two girls, she couldn't believe it – she was early! Then out of nowhere, Vicky and her mum appeared.

"She had to bring her mum, didn't she," Jane muttered sarcastically under her breath but she forced herself to smile as Vicky skipped over to her.

"Have you seen Clara yet?" Vicky asked.

"No," Jane replied flatly.

"Ok. No need to take it out on me." Vicky shot back.

A few minutes later, Clara arrived.

"Hi Jane, Hello Vicky," Clara said and greeted them with a smile.

A bell rang to signal the start of the fireworks which was followed by a loud bang and pink sparks cascading into the air. The firework display had begun.

Vicky's mum stood silently, her eyebrows raised, clearly unimpressed by the marvellous display in front of her.

"Close your mouth dear, it'll catch flies." she snapped. Vicky's mouth shut at the speed of light. "This is terribly boring. Come on Vicky, I'm going home."

Vicky felt a surge of anger inside her. It was utterly unfair for her mum to boss her about like that. She felt confident. More confident than she had ever been.

"No, Mum." She replied.

"Call me Mother, you know I hate it when you call me 'mum'. What do you mean 'no'?"

"You go home I'm staying right here." Vicky said confidently.

"Fine, then you stay and waste your time watching this ghastly rubbish," Vicky's mum stormed off in a huff.

After ten minutes of brightly coloured Catherine Wheels and impressive Roman Candles it began to get a little windy. A bright orange Catherine Wheel went up and a huge gust of wind dragged it along the night sky. It flew along and exploded above Vicky's house.

A couple of minutes later an ambulance arrived, the siren screeching like an angry cat. As it passed the park, Vicky saw who was in it, it was her mum.

Chapter 8

Run. That was all David Peterson needed to do, run. He had crept through Prendergast Avenue, hid in Knightly Lane and now he was running for his life.

David Peterson sold faulty fireworks illegally and now the police were after him. He had sold dangerous Catherine Wheels to the council and someone had found out, but David's legs were giving up. He decided he needed to find somewhere to rest, and fast. He couldn't just sit down on a bench, he needed to hide for the night. Watterson Road was full of abandoned houses. There were plenty of houses with windows smashed or broken doors for him to hide in but David was a fussy man. He had left his home in Bath when he was sixteen and was used to servants feeding him and doing anything he wanted them to do. He couldn't bear the thought of sleeping in a house with no silk sheets or satin pillows.

Then he came across one of the most magnificent and elaborate houses he had ever seen. The roof had fallen in and the door was smashed to pieces. But it still looked so nice, so comfortable, so posh...

He crawled in through the remains of the door and inspected his new home. The third floor had fallen down and the second floor was severely damaged but the ground floor was perfectly intact. Expensive paintings covered the walls and white china vases sat on mahogany tables. A crystal chandelier hung from the ceiling and a magnificent cream armchair was perched in the corner of the room. David sat down on it and rubbed his sore feet. This is where he would live for the next few months –

or at least until the police came. He would live off all the food in the house and sleep in the silk sheets. Or so he thought...

Chapter 9

The phone rang. This was the only noise that could be heard in the police station and Bob Anders (who was used to sitting in silence every day) answered it almost immediately.

"Good morning, PC Anders speaking, how may I help you?"

"Good morning indeed, I've spent the whole morning tidying up my garden, fixing my broken roof and repainting my door, that is NOT what I call a good morning!" the phone screamed at him.

PC Anders was shocked. He thought that all cases were about kittens stuck up trees and people robbing banks - not angry residents complaining that they were having a bad day.

"Well... er... is there any way I can help?"

"There are plenty of things you can do to help; I thought you were supposed to be a policeman for goodness sake!"

This put a tear in Bob's eye. He had finished university with dreams of being a member of the police force but his lack of experience had destroyed his hopes of being an important member of the police. Instead of a smart blue uniform, he was given a tatty old cap and a badge and he ended up in a grubby old office in London. Now he was more determined than ever to fulfil his duty as a police officer.

"What caused this mayhem ma'am?" he asked, drawing himself to his full height.

"The firework display of course!"

The policeman thought to himself. He had heard of a man selling faulty fireworks the previous week, he needed to track him down.

"Don't worry ma'am, I'm on the case!"

Chapter 10

Vicky had not spoken since she heard the news that her mother was in hospital. She kept telling herself that it was her fault and that it wouldn't have happened if she had just listened to her. It wasn't of course. Her mother had been reading when a firework had brought down the roof of her house and she was taken to hospital a few minutes later.

It had nothing to do with Vicky, and Clara and Jane were desperate to convince her of it.

"We've got to do something," exclaimed Clara. "Vicky hasn't spoken since the firework display!"

"I know, I'm a little worried too. Maybe if we go to the den it might take her mind off everything, she's always happy in the den!" Jane replied.

"Good idea."

They found Vicky on a bench, staring into space. She looked up at them, sighed, and let her head drop back down again.

"Vicky, are you alright?" Clara asked softly.

"Of course she's not alright, her mum is in hospital!" Jane muttered.

Clara gave her a look.

"Look Vicky, it's not your fault what happened last week. You should be glad your mum isn't dead. Mary Green who runs the bakery got knocked by a car last week. She was killed instantly!" Jane said, becoming more agitated by the second.

"She could die," replied Vicky, nearly crying.

"You're not helping!" hissed Clara in Jane's ear.

Jane's face softened.

"I'm sorry Vicky, please forgive me for being insensitive." said Jane.

Vicky smiled at the sight of Jane Thomas begging for forgiveness, in fact, it was so funny that Vicky laughed. It was the first laugh in what seemed like years. Jane smiled triumphantly.

"I forgive you," replied Vicky, trying to stop laughing. Clara burst out laughing.

"What are you two laughing about?" Jane snapped, but soon she started laughing too. In no time at all, the three friends were laughing together like they had done many times before.

"I think that it's a good idea to go to the den, what do you say fellow ladies, shall we?" questioned Clara.

Clara and Jane looked longingly at Vicky. Vicky smiled.

"Of course!"

It was a short walk to Vicky's house and they were there before they knew it.

"Here we are," exclaimed Vicky, pushing the door open. The three girls gasped.

Standing there in the corner of the den was a man. A man whose face was patched with mud and trousers covered in rips.

Clara was appalled, Jane was shocked but Vicky was curious.

"Who on earth are you?" she asked.

Clara opened her mouth to scream.

"Please don't scream," the man begged.

"Why shouldn't I?" she replied, forgetting her manners for once.

"I tell you what, if you don't scream, I'll… I'll… I'll be your slave!" he blurted out desperately.

"Is that all?" asked Jane.

"Wait! If you don't scream, I'll tell you my story, who I am and what's happened to me until now. I'll tell you everything!"

Vicky's curiosity got the better of her.

"It's a deal!" she cried. Clara glared at her but she had no choice, she had to keep her mouth shut, but this was easier said than done.

Chapter 11

Clara's eyes were wide in awe. David Peterson had told a true story more exciting than any fictional story that anyone could ever read. He had run away from his father after an argument and had hidden in an old warehouse. He had overheard something he shouldn't have but he wouldn't tell the three girls what it was about, not yet anyway. He had stolen faulty fireworks from the warehouse and had sold them in an attempt to make some money but his plan had gone horribly wrong. He had managed to sell some fireworks to the London council but the police weren't fools, not all of them anyway.

But the council were adamant to make the most of their money. They didn't have any more money to buy more fireworks so they had to use the faulty ones. The firework displays had caused many problems in Clara's neighbourhood, since all the gunpowder landed there, but still the council wouldn't budge. Vicky was amazed.

"So all those faulty fireworks were from you?" she asked.

"Yes, and I'm ashamed of it too," David replied, sighing.

"I hope so!" interrupted Jane. "Our lives have completely changed thanks to you!"

"But change isn't always a bad thing," said Clara who (amazingly) had remained silent and sat in the back of the den, not doing anything, just thinking. David lifted his head.

"No, it isn't," he remarked. "Change happens - it's a part of life and it always will be." It was something his father had said and saying it made him realise that he missed him more than he thought. David saw a light out of the corner of his eye. His eyes widened. Clara sent an alarming look at Jane to get her to hide the star but it was too late. It was in his hands but he was examining it with care.

"Do you know what this is?" he cried. "It's the pole star!"

"How do you know so much about stars?" asked Jane warily. David became quiet.

"What was the secret you overheard in the warehouse?" Vicky questioned, breaking the silence.

David remained quiet.

"I think you've got some explaining to do!" laughed Clara.

David gave in. He told them about the two astronauts at the warehouse. They were talking about stars. Every so often, a star falls out of the sky. No one usually notices because fairies send them back up with a shower of fairy dust, but if a star stays on earth for more than 105 days, the star will die, killing the earth with it.

"But I don't understand why the star landed on earth, what happened to the fairy?"

Clara showed him the corpse.

"Hmmnn, interesting - the high increase of oxygen must have killed the fairy before it could send the star back up.

"Huh?" Jane asked.

Clara and Vicky laughed.

"Wait, what will happen to us? We've had the star for 10 weeks now- that's only 5 weeks left!" cried Clara.

"What are we going to do?" asked Vicky.

A fierce look came over David's face.

"I don't know- but we're going to do something, that's a promise!"

Chapter 12

"Do I have to?" moaned Jane, sitting herself down on an old cardboard box.

Clara fixed her with a cold stare.

"Ok, ok, I'll do it!" she replied quickly, for she did not want a lecture from Clara Jones.

Jane was not a fan of gardening but with a little nagging from Clara, she eventually got the job done.

"See, that wasn't so bad," said Clara cheerfully.

This time, Jane gave her a look.

But Jane had indeed done a good job. Rose buds sat neatly in rows along the edge of the den, and pansies littered the entrance.

David had stayed with the three girls for 3 weeks now and he was beginning to glue the girls together. Vicky had told everyone that her father was looking after her so as not to arouse suspicion, even though he was away on a business trip.

"Good morning girls, I trust you had a good night," David exclaimed, stretching his arms.

"It's about time! It is 1:15pm, we all woke up at 8:00am!" declared Clara.

"Well I am indeed truly sorry for any mishap I may have caused," replied David.

"I am indeed truly sorry!" mimicked Jane, who burst into laughter.

"Jane!" screeched Vicky, shocked.

"Alright everyone, calm down" sighed Clara. "It's nearly time."

Chapter 13

Two weeks passed. The sky was blue and the sun was shining.

"This may be the last day we ever see the sun again," sighed Clara.

"Don't be so pessimistic, David says that the plan can't fail!" replied Jane. Vicky said nothing. She was sitting on the grass, staring up at the sky. Her eyes were bright with excitement. She wasn't worried - or even slightly nervous, she didn't have a care in the world.

The day flew by as quickly as it had arrived. The shimmering golden sun had soon become the cold silver moon.

"It's eight o'clock, we've got four hours to save the world," muttered David.

"Well what are we waiting for?" said Vicky at last. "Who cares if we don't manage to save the world, the last 5 weeks have been the most amazing of my life. We've become a family, and families stick together."

Jane was the first to speak.

"You're right Vicky."

David nodded. All eyes were on Clara.

Clara sighed. "It's impossible."

Vicky's head dropped.

"But I'm willing to give it a go."

Chapter 14

"Are you ready?" whispered Clara.

"I was born ready," replied Vicky.

"THREE!" shouted David.

Jane took a deep breath.

"TWO!"

Clara closed her eyes.

"ONE!"

Vicky smiled. It was time.

"Look!" exclaimed Jane.

Five candles were lit around the dead fairy and they began to flash. Slowly but surely they began to grow brighter. All of a sudden, the fairy began to shimmer. It gently opened its eyes. Jane gasped.

"I told you it would work!" smiled David.

Gradually, the fairy began to rise. It said nothing. It flew over to the star. In a cascade of gold, the star began to float upwards.

"Incredible!" whispered David.

"Indeed!" replied Vicky.

The star and the fairy spiralled slowly into the sky. The twinkle of light grew fainter and fainter as they disappeared into the night.

A dazzling light shone over the town. Everyone fell into deep sleep...

Clara was the first to wake up. Could it be? Could morning have arrived? She smiled and gazed at the silent world around her. The plan had worked.

Jane woke up next.

"Good morning Clara," she yawned. "Did we really do it, did we save the world? Or was it just a dream, a remarkably amazing dream?"

"If it was a dream, I dreamt it too!"

"It wasn't a dream," said David. "It truly did happen!"

Vicky woke up last.

"We did it, we saved the world!" The three friends hugged each other. They didn't notice a tall figure leaving the den. It was time for David to go.

Epilogue

So what happened to those remarkable three girls I hear you ask, well, life went back to normal for Clara, Jane and Vicky, but as all children must, they grew up, and never saw each other again.

Clara became a teacher. She was firm with the children, yet she listened to them. She was well respected by all who met her.

Jane became an artist. She studied art in university and moved to Paris. She has lived there ever since. She painted landscapes and portraits, but most of all she painted stars. She sat and painted the sky at night, as this was her favourite thing to paint.

As for Vicky, the curious, lonely little girl. Her mother came out of hospital, a changed woman. She didn't care about wealth any more.

Vicky studied English and eventually became an author. At first, she wrote about fantasy, about tales of magic and mayhem but then she started writing about reality. She wrote about unlikely people forming families, about people being alone, about the truth. Before she died, she wrote a biography of her childhood, which was never published.

I found that biography after she died and read it. I found her story incredible and couldn't resist writing about it.

That is what you have just been reading. □

www.ingramcontent.com/pod-product-compliance
Lightning Source LLC
Chambersburg PA
CBHW071223130626
46555CB00004B/1827